Bread&Milk
and other stories

Bread&Milk
and other stories

Eileen Gibbons Kump

Brigham Young University Press

Library of Congress Cataloging in Publication Data

Kump, Eileen Gibbons, 1927–
  Bread and milk, and other stories.

  I. Title.
PZ4.K96472Br [PS3561.U445]   813'.5'4   79-15754
ISBN 0-8425-1702-2
Brigham Young University Press, Provo, Utah 84602
© 1979 Brigham Young University Press. All rights reserved
Printed in the United States of America.
79 5Mc 40724

To
Ferrell
 and our children: Charlotte, Rodney Dean,
 Nancy, and Amy

Contents

Prologue ix
The Willows 1
China Doll 17
Jephthah's Daughter 27
Regarding Courtship 37
Bread and Milk 53
Four and Twenty Blackbirds 61
Sayso or Sense 71
God Willing 81

Prologue

From a log house in a clearing in the woods of Nelson Township, Portage County, Ohio. From New Lisbon, Osage County, New York, and from the shores of the Wabash and Erie Canal. From South Hope, Huron, Canada, and across the ocean from New Brunswick, England. From Booneville and Plymouth.

Lives converged, drawn together by that religious phenomenon in Kirtland, Ohio: Joseph Smith the Prophet. All were drawn into a drama that took them and their convert zeal to Missouri, to Nauvoo, to the Salt Lake Valley. Zion. And then out again into a wheel of settlements reaching every extremity of Deseret.

From one permanent dwelling after another they moved until their lives converged in one long narrow valley with thirsty soil. Here the dynamic, hurt-ridden beginnings of Mormonism quieted into more ordinary struggles for survival, perfection, and the rearing of righteous children away from a wicked world.

The Amy of these stories was born in that valley in 1876, granddaughter of those original converging lives, product of strength acquired in persecution, plain-crossing, and in finally settling somewhere for good. Her own fifty grandchildren, twentieth-century Mormons and for the most part still exuberant about their religion, heard Amy tell of an ancient-sounding time and place where plural marriage and May Day celebrations were common but cement basements and money in the pocket were ideas too far-fetched to be comprehensible.

I am one of those grandchildren. The stories in this volume were written out of the rich vein of practicality and resilience demonstrated by Grandma's generation of pioneers. They must be called fiction, I suppose, because so much of them is made up. After all, I wasn't there to hear Amy boss her brother Will or lovingly lecture her dead husband. That doesn't mean that the stories aren't true. They are. They could have happened as well as what happened. And I wrote them gratefully.

The Willows

Amy was a child when Congress passed the Edmunds Bill, assuring the end of polygamous living in Utah, but she was old enough to know that Aunt Edna was not her aunt at all but Will's mother and that Will was her favorite brother even though he was three years younger than she was and therefore not quite an equal. And when the heavy snows of 1884 had melted up north allowing the U.S. marshals through to do their duty in the south, when fear hung around their hunted mothers and fathers like weeping willows, she and Will still had to bundle their dolls and dishes in the green scarf and go to the orchard.

As they walked, Amy poked Will hard.

"I looked already," he growled.

"Did not!"

Amy knew he liked to watch his toes nuzzle the dust but she also knew that looking up was a lot more exciting than looking down because red hills wiggle under hot sun. Besides, God probably watched over from up there. Probably he did. That high he could even see Pa and the secret place.

Will followed Amy in and out of the young trees that grew down the middle of town. They saw a woman out on the porch bending over her big wooden tub. Of course they did not stop. You could tell when a mother pretended to look but did not really look at what she was doing that it was not a good day to visit. The children walked slowly past and Amy poked Will every time he forgot to look up.

The cooper shop was still empty. Amy ran toward the closed door and slid her fingers along four new churns. Every day they felt smoother, rounder, newer. Oh, she hoped they would sit there forever! But the wish was a stone in her stomach and she tugged at Will to hurry.

By the time Amy and Will got to the orchard, the Sevy boys were up a plum tree. Amy frowned in their direction and let go a long groan. This had been a perfect place, private and perfect. She and Will had cleared away rocks and bee weeds. They had even dug themselves their own pile of dirt. The trees spread shade big enough to sit in and nearby was City Creek for mud-making. Amy made up her mind that she would not leave and she would pay no notice to the Sevys.

Amy and Will crouched side by side over a dirt house, their small hands shaping, smoothing, caressing. Their real houses were just alike but Will's ma had planted sweet peas along each side of her broad plank walk. In Amy's dooryard there was only violet tamarisk.

Amy was pushing a twig into her tiny yard when a green plum struck the dirt house. She glared upward at four dangling legs.

"Damn, that was a fine one!" shouted Fred Sevy.

"Damn, this is a fine one, too!" yelled Phil.

Amy couldn't stand it. Not only did the Sevy boys have a pa who walked down the street in broad day but they said swear words in a painless way that made Amy shudder and tingle at the same time. Clamping a hand tight over each ear, she threw back her head and stuck out her tongue.

"Gentiles!"

Then she looked at Will. He had become worshipful. He bent toward her and put his mouth against her ear. "I hate them Sevys," he whispered.

Amy cupped her hand around his ear and whispered back, "They are gentiles, Will. Both of them."

"We hate gentiles," he said. "We hate 'em!"

Amy nodded twice, long and slow, looking Will right in the eyes the whole time. Then she sat up straight and began to pat and mold the dirt house as if nothing had happened.

"I forgot. Pa said we don't hate anybody. Not even the Sevys. Now let's play." Sometimes Amy got tired explaining, but there were some things even a five-year-old ought to know. Of course there were big folks' secrets they were too little for, like why John Saunders disappeared into Red Canyon every afternoon with a lunch basket and a water keg, or why the brethren took lookout turns on top of the canyon wall. At first sight of the marshal's buggy a boulder would come crashing down. Of course little children were too young to know that.

But Will still leaned toward her, whispering, waiting. "The Sevys swear, huh."

"Gentiles don't know better," Amy said.

"Why don't they?"

"Because they're gentiles." Amy had heard Brother Swenson tell Pa when the Sevys moved in that Mr. Sevy was one, so likely it had to do with not going to meetings or building uneven fences or letting your beard go.

"What is a gentile?" asked Will, his voice way above a whisper now.

"Something going to hell!" yelled Phil Sevy. "Something going right down to hell, dammit!" A splatter of wet pits hit Will square in the face and he was instantly on his feet, red-faced and funny looking because the knees of his overalls caked into bends even though he stretched on tiptoe. He did not wait for Amy to come up with another of her wonderful words that wasn't swearing.

"You—you muh-gar-ries you!" he screamed. "You mean old muh-gar-ries!"

Amy caught herself or she would have fallen right over at the sound of that word. She could not have heard what she thought she heard! Not said aloud, shouted even. And not from Will! Why, he was a child! She had been almost eight when she was told about McGary!

"They are muh-gar-ries, aren't they, Amy?"

But she had heard. There he went again.

"Shhh," she said. "Shhh!"

She could not think what to do and there was nobody to ask. Aunt Edna would probably scold Will good.

"Will Taylor!" she said, "What do you know? You tell me right now what you know."

"He's bad."

"You never saw him, I bet!"

"I didn't see him, but Ma said she'd tie knots in his beard and yank it out." Will leaned so close to Amy that his mouth made her ear wet. "You seen him?"

Amy stiffened and rubbed her ear. "Course I have, almost. And I bet Aunt Edna didn't say that either." Amy had heard her own mother say she would like to put some epsom salts in the marshal's mush, but somehow Aunt Edna's threat was better. Did she really want to hurt him? Was he wicked? Maybe he was a gentile like the Sevys. She could see

Aunt Edna stretching on her tiptoes, reaching but unable to touch the bigness with just the tip of its huge beard showing.

"Aunt Edna wouldn't say that so you could hear!"

"She did, though. She did honest, Amy," pleaded Will.

Amy still doubted it, but she was weary with envy and disappointment and her voice fell. "You're too little to talk about McGary, Will, let alone see him. Besides, if you saw him you might have to lie, and you can't even lie yet."

"Could you lie?"

Amy felt old and wise again as she watched Will's eyes grow big and his mouth slowly come open. "Sure I could. Most of the big kids can. But Addie Smith can't, and she's ten. One day she almost told."

"What did she tell?"

"Where her pa was, of course. Anyway, she sure got it, too." Amy handed Will two small tin cups and wrapped the wooden dolls in the green scarf. She could suddenly think of nothing but Pa. He was somewhere for sure, somewhere high, and he missed her too probably. Pa—

"We shouldn't talk about it, Will," she said. "Come on, let's play Salt Lake City."

Will obeyed, as always, and with a few quick stamps of his bare feet the house was flattened. He ran to the creek with cups and then watched in awe as Amy molded mud into disks the exact size of the tin saucers. As always happened when Will was delighted with her, he giggled as he watched. She handed one saucer to Will and took the other between small hands red with dirt.

"We better play or it will be supper time and we'll have to go. You be the pa and I'll be the ma."

"Where's the other ma?" yelled Phil Sevy. "Mormons can't have just one ma!"

"This is only play, Phil Sevy, so you shut up!"

"You shut up," echoed Will bravely.

"Shhh, Will," said Amy. "Remember what I told you."

The magic of mud pies and the frown with which Will played the papa withdrew Amy completely from thoughts of McGary and the swearing Sevys. She lifted her cup with her fingers instead of her whole hand and she talked fine. Soon she was in Salt Lake City and, in her finest cape and manners, chatting over store pastries.

The warning sound broke Amy's make believe into a million pieces. There was the sudden clap of rock against rock, of something hurling its way down the mountain. It was not a loud sound but it might as well have broken the earth right in two. Amy sat motionless, staring down the road past the trees and the silent shops and the empty porches and knowing there was nobody in the world except her and Will.

"Here comes McGary," yelled the Sevy boys as they leaped from their tree and sped laughing up the road. "Run, Mormons, run! Run from the black buggy! Run to Arizona!"

Amy did not move.

"They're just foolin, aren't they, Amy? Who is muh-gar-rie, huh?" whispered Will.

Amy tried hard to enjoy being eight and knowing. Her whole self hurt to tell Will all about it. But of course she must not, and she must hide, and hide Will, too, and not tell. They ought to hide somewhere right now!

"He's coming, Will. He's coming around the east bend right now." She thought about Pa and about Addie Smith almost telling and she wished she was with her mother at the mill. But Mama would not be at the mill. By now she would be hid. If she had heard the boulder she would be safe by now. *If she heard the boulder—*

Suddenly Amy was on her feet and running. "Ma's at the mill! She's tending the mill and she won't hear," Amy shouted back. "You better go somewhere so McGary won't ask you things!" Amy's bare feet sank in the soft earth along the ditchbank like wooden spoons in new butter and the tall grass sliced at her legs. The wooden plank slapped against her feet when she crossed Lund's dooryard and she stumbled over a hoe in the ploughed field where she had dropped potatoes that very morning. Without slowing, she ran the long trail up the mill, the trail that no amount of walking could pack hard. Here and there rocks had been bared and rounded, but the earth had remained sand soft.

"Ma!" Amy screamed as she ran through the mill. "Ma!" Her voice sounded hollow in the empty room. She found Lee Robertson out back waiting for flour. "Where's Ma?"

"She's hid, thank God."

God! Of course! He would help! He had brought them Aunt Edna and he had saved Pa's life when he got poisoned with sheep dip!

"Where did God hide her?"

But Lee didn't say. Instead he stiffened and looked past Amy. At the sound of a boot against the wooden floor, she whirled, almost backing into the water wheel. The boot belonged to a body that filled the doorway. It was in Sunday clothes, nice ones, and behind it at the end of the path was a black-topped buggy. Across the road stood the Sevy boys, half smiling, pale.

"Where's the miller?" The marshal looked at Lee, then at Amy. She swallowed hard two times and tried to stand tall. She tried to see the knives and pistols big kids said were hidden in the beard that lay on McGary's black vest. But the beard was no bigger than Pa's and it was combed.

"You're a pretty little thing, aren't you?"

Amy backed up another step.

"How old are you?"

"Pa's gone."

The big man squatted and smiled. His voice was gentle. His eyes, almost buried in bushes of eyebrows, were kind. "I just want to talk to him," he said.

"Pa isn't around," Amy said. Maybe she wouldn't get to lie. Pa hadn't been home since the night Zephyr was born and the only way she had known he was home then was by going outside and peeking through a tear in the blind.

"Where is he?"

"Pa's been gone a long time. I don't know where."

"Who runs the mill?"

Amy hesitated. "Ma."

McGary's face brightened. "Well, I'd like to see your mother. Where is she?"

"I don't know."

The eyes turned. They looked slowly around the room and Amy wondered as McGary stood how Aunt Edna could even think of hurting anyone so big. He hurried through the mill, looking everywhere. Suddenly he seized a sack of grist and threw it against the wall. "Damn cohabs," he muttered. *"Damn smart cohabs."*

Amy moved behind Lee. Cohabs! A new word! A new word that might not be swearing!

"Your bird has flown," said Lee. Amy felt brave behind him, and she thought the way he said things exactly right.

McGary's face was dark and worried as he came toward Amy again. He squatted once more and looked into her eyes. "Are you sure you don't want to tell me where your folks are?"

Amy shook her head. "I don't know where."

McGary stood up and looked across at Lee before hurrying out the door. "This is a hell of a mill to run without a miller, young man." He ran down the path.

Lee laughed as he took his full sack of flour from the mill. "You sure got spunk, Amy Taylor. Weren't you scared?"

Amy could not answer. She sat in the doorway and watched the buggy go. By the time it was out of sight her insides ached and she noticed her legs were shaking.

"Your ma's at the willows. She's safe enough," said Lee. "McGary won't likely be back today now he knows we've outsmarted him again."

The Willows

Amy knew that Lee meant she might as well go home, and she started down the trail. Slivers from the mill floor stung as her feet spread the warm sand and she did not know why but her eyes suddenly stung too and made tears that tasted sandy and salty, and then she was running again, through her own mother's dooryard and garden spot, past the tithing house, along Swenson's fence and under it. Across the wide field lay a sea of green willows, taller than tamarisk and almost as thick where their clumps began. Long ago when Pa broke his leg she had gathered the long saplings and sat for hours watching him weave baskets. The firmest and greenest willows he kept out to slit and tap into whistles.

As Amy slid into them, the willows gave way, falling wide. Amy moved quickly, tearfully, among the tiny clearings. In each, two or three women sat, their knees drawn up to make an arm rest or to make room for someone else. Mary Swenson was crying, her head back, eyes shut as if she were at prayers. One old woman stitched on patches. Aunt Edna was looking straight ahead as if she were thinking about her sweet peas. The black curls on her forehead were wet.

Amy stopped. There were so many women. But when she finally saw her mother seated alone among the thickest willows she ran and fell into her lap.

"Ma! Ma!" The tears were gone and Amy's heart leaped. "I saw him, and I almost lied, and he's got a combed—"

"Amy!" The single word and her mother's strong arms jerked Amy to her feet and then two coarse hands held her face tight between them. Strands of her mother's long hair, usually piled smooth and shiny, hung loose around the browned cheekbones that looked to Amy like fists.

"Amy Taylor, you ought to be whipped!" The hands were too tight against Amy's face. "How old are you, Amy?" The hands shook her and the eyes in which Amy had read so many nice things were different than she had ever seen them. "Are you five years old?"

"I'm eight. Will's five."

"Then go right home, and don't ever, ever look for me again!" The hands turned her but held on. "What would we do if Pa had to go away and not come back? What if Aunt Edna and her children all went?" Then the hands pushed.

Amy slipped from the willows. Will could not go away. Some of the children and mothers had disappeared, but Will would not. Pa might go to jail though if she did not remember she was eight. How would it be different for Pa to be away in jail instead of away hiding? Some way it would be different. Amy slid slowly under the fence. Her tears made pebbles in the dry earth as she tried to fit the woman in the willows inside the mother who talked about Pa as if he were God. She tried to remember the excitement and the new word, but her cheeks still burned and her head was fuzzy inside. When Pa got angry, he thumped her head with his big thumbnail. Ma did not get angry.

As Amy turned the corner of the tithing house, she heard a noise behind her and looking back she saw her mother in the shadow of the building. "There's bread and milk in the coolroom, Amy. Maggie is at Aunt Edna's so you put the babies to bed."

It was black outside by the time Amy had set the milk and bread back in the coolroom and convinced Ben that Ma would be in bed with him when he woke up. She rocked Zephyr until she slept, then climbed into the corner bunk that hung suspended by big ropes laced through holes in the wall. She sank deep into the mattress to wait for Maggie. The moon stared through a knothole just like the eye of a coyote, and she wished Maggie would hurry up.

Amy wasn't sure what woke her, whether it was the talking or the quickly moving feet or the light ridging the door, but her father's voice, low and flowing, became suddenly clear. She slid from the bunk, opened the kitchen door, and slipped inside. Aunt Edna was rushing back and forth and so was Ma, like they did when they bottled or got ready for a picnic. The table was piled high with things Amy barely saw because there, sitting in front of the fireplace with his back to her, was Pa. She stared at the big bent shoulders, wanting to climb right over them into the lap. But her mother's voice came anxiously.

"Get into bed, Amy. Please."

Pa turned so fast that Amy fell against the door, startled. He smiled at her and before she could even smile back he reached out and picked her up. He drew her tightly against the big buttons, the rough shirt, and held her. The chair began to tip back and forth, to the edge of a squeak but not full on it. Warm in the fire, unbearably happy, Amy did not say anything for a long time. Then she started wishing Will was there, too. It was wrong, him not knowing. Amy curled there, remembering Will and McGary. She could hardly stand it. She must not talk. She must act her age.

But the squirms could not be helped finally and she was sitting up, pushing herself loose and looking into Pa's face. His hair was not as black as it had been and the beard that had shamed all other beards in town when Pa babied it was too long. But the eyes were the same.

"You're every bit as big as McGary, I bet," Amy said.

"Bigger," said Pa. "With the Lord, I'm bigger." He spoke softly and squeezed her again and Amy laughed and was bubbly inside at the sound of Pa's voice.

"I saw McGary today," said Amy. "And I didn't tell him anything." She waited for Pa to reply but he just pulled her against him. "Will and me were at the orchard alone when the rock fell." Pa didn't seem to be listening. He lifted her high and carried her back toward the bunk. "McGary begged me to tell, Pa, but I remembered!"

When Pa laid her down, she felt the big hands with their softening callouses slip back over her forehead to the tips of her braids. He kissed her cheek. She must not ask questions. She must not. But she touched his sleeve. "Will you be here when I wake up?"

"Not this time. I've got to play hide and seek with Brother McGary a little longer." Pa stood for a long time looking about him, then stepped over to Zephyr's crib and straightened the quilt.

"Go back to sleep, Amy." Pa shut the door behind him.

Amy lay for a long time hearing the voices and trying to see Pa move through the light around the door. Why had Pa come and why didn't Aunt Edna and Mama act happier about it? If he was *Brother McGary,* was he good? How could that be? He had to be bad. But there were no knives and pistols in his beard. She was sure of that.

Daylight usually teased Amy awake, but morning was full on her face before she woke. She and Will might not have time for a single make-believe before she had to drop potatoes! As she dressed she listened for Will outside. He would be calling her. Then suddenly there were footsteps moving along the porch. Good. Mama was home. As Amy pulled on her dress she could hardly wait to see Will's eyes grow big and his mouth flop open when she told him the new word that McGary had said. It didn't sound like swearing. Probably it wasn't.

She stepped out the door into the shade of the tamarisk at the foot of the rise separating Aunt Edna's house from her mother's. "Will!" She waited. When he didn't burst out the door and run toward her, she climbed on, calling again, much louder than she had intended. She stepped to the porch. "Will!" Aunt Edna would scold her for sure for being unladylike.

The door of the house was ajar. Amy stepped inside. The rooms were empty. Except for the wash bench and a table and the black stove, the house was bare. Even the corn husk beds were gone and the ladder to the garret where Will slept lay on the floor. Beside it, bundled around the dolls and dishes, was the green scarf. Amy's heart pounded. Will didn't know hardly anything! But he was gone and so was

Aunt Edna and Emma and baby Seth. And so was the oval mirror from Salt Lake City.

Amy wanted to run down the hill to Ma. She would know all about it. Mama!

But she must not ask. She thought about Pa's shirt that scratched and tickled her face. She must help. She must lie and she mustn't ask Mama questions, no matter what. She must remember she was eight.

Picking up the scarf of toys, she walked outside and sat on the edge of the porch, pushing her toes into the dust the way Will did and feeling as if she would burst with things about Pa and McGary and cohabs. Slowly and tenderly she undid the chain of knots Will had tied around their toys and laid the dolls and dishes in a neat row. She tried to make believe, but she kept hearing the Sevys laughing from the trees and she kept seeing Ma in the willows and feeling her strong hands. Damn Sevys. The words pushed to come out but could not. "I guess I won't play," she said aloud, as if she hoped the dolls and dishes would not care. "I don't have a pa anyhow." She looked up and then she saw the shadow. McGary was standing in the back doorway of her mother's house, his face dark and worried again. Then he saw Amy and the face was not as dark and the legs moved toward her. Your bird has flown, McGary. As he came rapidly up the rise, his enormous silver belt buckle gathered light. Amy stood. The marshal's beard was combed but the marshal was a gentile. He had to be. She arched her back against the porch post and waited.

China Doll

Knowing how life is, Harriet was skeptical, but again this morning warm wings of excitement hovered. Every morning since the day the family had come home from Grandpa's ranch, the wings had been almost more than she could bear. Not only had Grandpa's fields and orchards yielded far beyond what Seth could get their own sandy soil to produce, but Esther was almost well, healed by herbs and faith, and cool mountain air. They had returned from Grandpa's with abundance.

On shelves suspended from the coolroom ceiling, golden cheeses hung. Below were jars of apple and plum, and in the sand spring out back stood cedar kegs full of butter. Harriet thought of these things and of the potatoes and grain in the cellar. The family were ready for winter. They had food stored and even Amy's old gray cat had finally found its way back to their door. A summer of feasting on plump ranch mice had not permanently warped her loyalties after all.

"Did she follow our wagon marks all the way home, Mama?" Amy asked. Harriet shook her head. "No, she has a cat sense we don't. But as I see it, her return is just one more blessing coming to our family."

One more blessing. The warm wings flew up and Harriet pushed her feet against the floor. All that remained of baby Esther's burn was a tender place the size of Amy's palm. With patience, that would heal too, as memories do. It had seemed all right to make the baby a bed in the big rocker. There in the warmth of the fireplace, she could sleep while Harriet and Amy made soap out in the arbor. These two had discussed it and it had seemed all right. What brought them flying inside together was a startled cry, like glass breaking, and they had found Esther on the floor, her head touching red embers, the chair rocking.

Harriet had plunged for her baby but Amy was faster. It was Amy, not Harriet, who had cradled Esther in her arms while Brother Swenson prayed and applied the holy oil and while Seth told the Lord to let the baby sleep and if it was his will to make her well. Amy still held her when she finally did go to sleep. She had rocked her until it was dark outside and she herself had to be carried up to bed.

Remembering, Harriet told herself that some hurt was useless and ought to be put aside. Besides, the warm wings had folded and it was suppertime.

Harriet hummed softly as she lay the table. Under each turned bowl she put a wild rose. She got the cheese and milk while Amy cut the bread and then the family knelt for prayers. "Thank him for the cat," she whispered to Seth.

Their bowls were almost empty and only Ben's plate still held its square of cheese (he liked to smell it even more than he liked to eat it), when there came a knock at the door. Harriet looked toward the sound.

"Who could that be?"

As Seth stood, the children swarmed for a look. Seth turned the knob and pulled. There before them, like daylight against darkness, stood a stranger wearing a white city outfit with even a bought hat. He smiled so hard and so well that Harriet feared for them all.

"Come inside," said Seth, putting out his hand.

But in one fist the stranger waved bright yellow handbills and in the other bright red tickets. Shaking hands was out of the question. "How would you like to spend the most exciting evening of your life?" asked the stranger, looking straight at the children. Their eyes followed his stuffed fists up and down and they nodded all together. The man gave Seth one of the yellow papers and he read the large print out loud slowly:

MARCUS THE MAGICIAN!
ONE NIGHT ONLY!
THE WORLD'S GREATEST SHOW!

Seth mumbled over the small print with his lips and said to hold still until he finished.

"There's no money here, sir," he said finally. He tried to give the paper back but the city man's hands were still full, and besides, he said, he wasn't fussy. His eyes circled the room and came to rest on Ben's plate. When he left, one of the big cheeses from the coolroom went with him.

"Food for worldly pleasure, Seth?" Harriet asked before the door had even shut behind the cheese. They were not as well fixed for the winter as they had been.

But the yellow paper said Marcus the Magician could stack nine chairs, one on top of the other, and balance them on his chin.

Perhaps it was an evening of worldly pleasure. But when it was over not even Harriet felt the urge to repent of it. There were the nine chairs, a store broom, and china cups and saucers she silently coveted and prayed would not break. Marcus drew live rabbits and pigeons out of a tall black hat and made them invisible. In fact, he made so many things disappear that after the beautiful lady vanished Seth whispered to Harriet that he might be an instrument of the devil. But the juggling came next and they forgot all about Satan and the Lady. The whole family for the whole evening thought only of magnificent Marcus, and when they got home Harriet slipped into the coolroom and hung lard where the cheese had been.

The next day when Amy took down the china doll Pa had brought her from Salt Lake City, Harriet's heart leaped with caution. It was too pretty. And it would break. But the words floated apart before she could say them and she put aside her sewing, and her fear, and watched the children. Ben and Maggie couldn't lift the kitchen chairs, let alone stack them, so they practiced vanishing instead. Amy fussed and giggled as she made the china doll a new white dress. She polished the black painted hair until it glistened. Then she picked up Esther and swirled around the room with her. "I love you too, my pet. I love you too."

Harriet spent all morning watching, wondering at the exhilaration that had invaded her home and her heart. She became restless, afraid, yet was giddy herself. It took cold, forced thought to break the spell. Magic was deceptive, artificial. Its pleasures had no wings but were brittle and silly.

Finally she spoke to Amy. She tried not to sound cross, though she felt cross, cross at Amy, who had outgrown dolls once, at Marcus the magnificent, who distorted life, and especially at herself, for not knowing exactly what to do.

"You had better put the china doll away, Amy. There's work." Harriet stood up and went into the kitchen.

Amy set the doll on its shelf, quickly, as if her mother's concern was something she should have felt herself. All afternoon she washed the clothes. Between scrubbings on the board Pa had made she tended Esther in the arbor. She even helped her to walk with only one hand clinging to the wash bench. Each time Esther fell, Amy picked her up and loved her. Of course, Esther did not hurt herself in the dense grass. Just once she fell against the bench, bumping the tender place. She whimpered that time but she didn't cry, and when the washing was done Amy held her until she went to sleep.

A few days later the flesh loosened and came off again. The color fled Esther's cheeks and Amy could not teach her walking any more. Seth and the brethren blessed Esther every day but Seth would not command the Lord, though Harriet asked him to, not for her own sake but for Amy's. Seth instructed God to do as he saw best, and Harriet watched and listened and yearned in her heart for Seth to be more firm. He should explain about Esther and Amy. Surely if God remembered the ordeal of Esther's birth and that Amy had heard it he would know that he mustn't take the baby back. Surely he must remember!

Never before or since that day had Harriet let the children see her cry. Always there had been time for them to be sent to the neighbors. This time Harriet was braiding Amy's hair when her labor began, abrupt and deep. Startled, Harriet let the braid drop. Her tears gathered and fell as Amy looked up at her and within minutes, though Harriet never wanted it, she was crying and gasping for help. As the midwife hurried into the yard, she had shoved Maggie and Ben toward her own place. "Don't worry about Amy," said Harriet, and Amy had stayed. She stood outside the bedroom door. She heard her mother's broken cries and the midwife's bewildering instructions.

When Amy saw Esther, red and ugly and strenuously alive even after such an ordeal, her heart divided.

Amy held Esther all night the last two days of her life. She was holding her when she died.

Seth made a pine box, and in the hills he found a large, smooth marker stone. Early the morning of the services he sat in the arbor chiseling an inscription. Beside him, Harriet knelt, her eyes following the movement of his hands. She did not see Amy approach.

"Mama?"

The voice sounded far away. Harriet did not look up. "Amy?"

"Mama, I decided to give Esther my china doll."

"What do you mean?"

"I'm going to put it in the casket. See, it's wearing the white dress."

Harriet raised her head only slightly. She turned it from side to side.

"But, Mama!"

"No," said Harriet. "It isn't necessary to do that, dear." Harriet looked up at her daughter then and saw that the eyes and the mouth had closed tight. She hoped that the heart had not closed too, but she must not think about that until tomorrow.

"Oh, Mama! Why? Please!"

Harriet leaned toward Seth's industry, then backward. She wanted to answer, though the girl should know by now that to understand is not always required.

"It's a china doll," said Harriet. She watched Amy's feet, unmoving, near. "Bury your wooden one if you want to, but where would we get another china doll?"

The feet moved and were gone. Harriet looked at the empty place where they had been and felt inexpressibly lonely.

Seth kept working. The tool still dug at the stone. "We didn't think we could spare the cheese either, Harriet," he said. "Couldn't we spare the doll?"

"To what use?"

"To Amy's use. She's young. She isn't as acquainted with life as we are."

"No, but she's begun!" Harriet felt the sudden flutter of hope in her breast, like tiny wings. "Amy's intelligent, Seth. She's grown up, thirteen already. She never fussed with that doll before the stage show. I want her to— Otherwise—" Harriet could not finish. She saw that the marker was finished and that her thought had vanished.

Seth laid down his tools and stood up. "Amy's fanciful. She's happy from inside out. Seems to me she grew up before she should have." He helped Harriet to her feet. "Next summer we'll make extra cheese. From now on we'll keep it on hand," he said. He laid the stone marker in the wagon and followed Harriet into the house to get the baby.

Jephthah's Daughter

Amy was on the plump side but she seldom thought about it. Even when she did, and right now was one of those painful times, her thoughts were not, as she saw them, vain and worldly. They would become vanity of course if she thought too much.

Beside her in the tall grass along the irrigation canal sat her closest friend. With no one else would Amy have even mentioned such a thing as looks.

"But you are good looking, Amy," said Lottie impatiently. "And you're not over plump." Lottie had long black hair that always fell in three perfect ringlets from the scoop on the crown of her head. She also had an exotic face with high cheekbones and dark eyes. And she had a beau. Oz Miller was so taken with her that he walked fences and swallowed hard boiled eggs in her presence.

Amy had no beau. Her hair looked better kept short and it was brown.

"It's easy for you to talk," said Amy. "You haven't a care." She took the paper from her pocket and together they read the rules for the fourth time:

> The queen of the May will have beauty. She will know how to weave and work and make good butter and salt rising bread. Her dress will be simple and will not imitate extravagant fashion. It will be of home manufacture. She will not take the name of Deity in vain nor speak lightly of Him. She will be devoted to the building up of the Kingdom of God.

The two girls looked at each other. Then with long sighs they flung themselves back in the grass, Lottie to stare into the furiously blue sky, Amy to shut her eyes tight against heaven. Her considerations were private. In her mind she put a shadowy finger over the sentence about beauty and saw the words through once more. Likely her bread was not good enough anyway. When she was not chosen it could be because of her bread. At weaving no one in her crowd was faster. Breadmaking was a weakness inborn and even if she were shapely like Lottie and even if she could be sure whether the committee meant beauty inside or beauty outside, there was the bread.

"I don't even want to be queen," she said out loud.

Lottie did not answer.

"Well, I don't!" she said, thrusting the paper back into her pocket and wadding it in her hand.

Slowly Lottie raised herself to one elbow and looked over at Amy with a weary expression that said she was oldest.

"Look, silly," she said, "everybody wants to be chosen." She waited for Amy to open her eyes. "I do. Only I'm not ashamed to admit it."

The earth opened wide enough for barely one and Amy felt herself disappear. The notion that Lottie Moffit could worry and want as Amy Taylor worried and wanted left Amy floating in fragments.

"You never said you wanted to be queen, Lottie!"

"Of course I do. Not as much as you do though. Nobody wants to be chosen as much as you do."

"That's a mean, cruel thing to say!"

"Well, it's true. It's as plain as pie and everybody knows it."

"They do not!"

Lottie smiled at her. "Look, Amy, it doesn't matter anyway. I am sure you will be chosen."

"Stop it, Lottie! Stop it!"

Half way home Amy broke the quiet between them. "You shouldn't say things like that, Lottie." But to herself she repeated and stored carefully away the prophetic words, recognizing them as friendship but hoping they were inspiration, hoping Lottie was right.

Lottie, walking beside her, knew she was. Amy Taylor was not the prettiest girl in town. She herself was. But Lottie Moffit would not win. Sometimes she did not wear the homespuns, and when she did she looked unnatural. She had even stepped with strangers now and then. The bare truth was simply that she was not admired the way Amy was and now that Amy was old enough to be queen, folks would show their approval of her by giving her that honor. Besides, the serious, industrious girl whose figure carried the vague suggestion of a dumpling was plenty good looking enough.

The bishop's committee in charge of May Day preparations did not ignore Amy's slight plumpness; rather, they counted it in her favor, Brother Thompson and Brother

Ingersoll asserting that it was essential to health and contentment in a woman. The female members of the committee, possessors of abundant health and content, applauded the good sense of the priesthood.

"She doesn't step yet, does she?" asked the chairman. All agreed that Amy appeared still free of light-headedness. After naming her queen, they chose twelve others, less exemplary but lovely just the same, to attend her. Lottie was one of these.

May Day morning, Amy arose before daylight and heated water for a leisurely bath before the oven door. Her best dress lay smoothed over a chair. Beside it, black slippers shone like enormous beetles in the lamplight. As she bathed, Amy sang the May Day song Sister Hunt had written especially for the program: "We crown you with these flowers, you merry queen of ours." So they had not really meant it about the bread! Or about beauty either? "Long life and happy years to come, tra la la la la la." Or had they? To be pretty—that would be something! A secret to surpass all secrets! Would Henry Jensen step her if she were plain? Of course not. She could hear Lottie say so. Yet, Henry Jensen was the handsomest, richest catch in the valley and it was a fact that he was escorting Amy to the May Day celebration.

Henry had caught up with her and Lottie at the flower gathering picnic up Red Hollow yesterday. She and Lottie had gone deep into the canyon for sand to scour knives and forks. Then they had climbed to the high rocks shelves where Indian skeletons and pottery had been found and had peered into caves and crumbling mud rooms. They had rolled down sand slopes and jumped from ledge to ledge where the canyon narrowed. Where Red Hollow ended and the steep sides nearly touched, Lottie's beau in a knightly performance had walked above their heads with a foot on each side of the deep red wedge. To Amy it showed he cared incredibly. She couldn't take her eyes off him.

"He'd die for you, Lottie."

"No he wouldn't."

"Oh, but he would!"

"Oz puts on. Boys like to act silly."

"Do you think he's silly for being brave?"

"Go find a lost cow, Lottie." Henry Jensen appeared from nowhere and Lottie flew down the canyon, Oz in pursuit.

"Cow? Whose cow?" Amy blushed. There was no cow. Henry Jensen laughed out loud but in such a gentlemanly way that Amy was able to smile back. He scooped a lavender blossom from its stem and with great flourish perched it among Amy's curls. "There! Now you look like the Queen of the May!"

Somehow the gesture reminded Amy of Oz Miller getting ready to swallow an egg. She quivered.

"Do you have an escort for the doings tomorrow?" Henry scooped one blossom after another from its stem and tossed it into Amy's bucket.

Amy shook her head. She tried to speak. She could tell him she was gathering sand instead of flowers. But her tongue had turned to a mitten in her mouth.

"A queen ought to have an escort," said Henry, and he went on tossing flowers.

Amy nodded her head this time. Then she wet the mitten as best she could. "I'm gathering sand instead of flowers."

"Sand!" Henry laughed again, but it was still a gentlemanly laugh. Does a queen gather sand on the eve of her coronation?" He kept picking flowers. "Let's hide the sand so no one will know. Come on. Help me." Amy tried to pick flowers too but hers clung to their stems.

"May I be your partner tomorrow, Amy?"

Her heart jumped once and was still.

"Yes," said the mitten. "Yes."

"Good," said Henry. "Now let's sit and rest." He talked an age then about getting her started in company and about what a good customer her pa was and how his own ma used white sand to scour. But only Amy's ears heard him. Although her heart had stopped beating, her brain had gone wildly ahead on its own. She was walking home from choir practice at his side and he was holding her hand.

By the time Henry had said goodbye and strode off down the canyon, she had planned a courtship that could only end in a proposal at Papa's knee in the comfortable Taylor parlor.

"But she's only fifteen, Henry!"

"I love her anyway."

Gone forever from one young bosom was the wispy fear that taunted every girl in town: Henry Jensen is sure to return from one of his trips to Salt Lake City with a wife.

By nine o'clock May Day morning every man, woman, and child in town was assembled on tabernacle square. Beside each tall straw hat was a broad, scooped oval one heaped with flowers. No one tried to corral the children. Gradually they would find their mothers' skirts and, clinging there, watch the spectacle.

In the clearing stood an even bigger maypole than last year's, its red, white, and blue streamers hanging free in the warm air. Nearby in their Sunday dresses sat the twelve attendants to the queen. Beside the bishop on a small platform sat Amy, and after the opening prayer she made her speech, thanking everyone for their kindness and promising to be a good queen, a good daughter to her mother and father, and a good daughter to God.

The Drama of Jephthah's Daughter, highlight of the whole day, came next. Every year the same tragedy was portrayed. Every year it broke every heart. Determined that today's performance would be the saddest in May Day history, Amy stepped from the platform and joined her friends. As she approached they sang to her as she had sung to herself in the tin tub before dawn, "We crown you with these flowers, you merry queen of ours. . . ." They placed a garland of flowers upon her head. "Now you look like the Queen of the May," Henry had said.

After the coronation Amy and her attendants surrounded the maypole, but they did not dance. As music suddenly swelled from the organ nearby, they sang of how Jephthah the Israelite was cast out of the city of Gilead by his brothers and how he came back to rule the Gileadites and be their victorious captain against the warring Ammonites. The music to this part of the program was a lively march and the girls sang with resounding rhythm of Jephthah's valor, his careless promise to God, and finally of his great victory.

After Jephthah's triumph the music stopped and quiet hung over the clearing. A delicate, unchorded melody played with one finger on the high keys began, and with its first lonely note Amy was no longer queen of the May but Jephthah's daughter. Her attendants were the daughters of Israel who were to roam and sing and dance with her until her time should come to be slain. "Let us go to the mountains," sang Amy. "Let us go to the mountains," sang the maidens. When at last they took their long strands of color, the organist played a waltz and they braided the maypole to portray their last, lovely times together.

For as many years as she could remember Amy had watched Jephthah's daughter and her maidens waltz around and around the maypole. And now the doing was even more beautiful than she had hoped. There beside Pa sat Henry Jensen smiling at her and she knew her white strand, like the widow's flour bin, would replenish itself forever in her hand.

When it did not, and the maypole stood suddenly wound, Amy realized that the waltz had become a mournful melody and that the time of Jephthah's daughter had come. Now Amy must touch every heart with her sorrow. She alone was responsible for every tear that fell, and if she failed, for those that didn't. She opened her mouth. The sad words came out. She did not forget one. But they were bubbling, tinkling things! Other years the last song of Jephthah's daughter had left Amy hurting all over. Today, Amy was agonized to discover that no matter how hard she tried she did not hurt at all! She, the chosen queen, was a disgrace to them all. She was a frivolous snipit, not a heroine! She was not being a good sacrifice even for the sake of the most moving part of the whole program!

As Amy walked slowly forward singing her last song and lay herself on the altar, worry lines crumpled her young forehead. Tears of disappointment flooded her eyes. And thus it came to pass that the expression she so feared would not be fitting was the most perfect in the history of May Day celebrations.

Regarding Courtship

Less than one week before Bryce Huntington was to marry his childhood sweetheart, she took typhoid and died. Although he was deeply hurt and for months would not be consoled by the fact that she waited for him in the heavens, he at last relented. Now, he considered eternity without his new sweetheart and discovered he wanted none of it unless she was there too.

Would she be? Bryce sat beside his betrothed in the porch swing, his mission call in his hand, and worried. The cold truth was plainly contrary to what he had understood God's mind to be, yet the evidence of divine opposition was surely there. God intended him, of all men, to remain a bachelor. The wedding date had been arranged when God sent this new delay: "Report to Salt Lake City and then travel to Boston." For at least two years Bryce was to preach the gospel, to put Amy out of his life. How could he do that? He put his arm around her and kissed her gently.

"If a man is married, it is different," he whispered. "I can think of you every day if we're married. Otherwise, you're only for holidays."

She moved closer to him.

"Please, Amy. Marry me now." He kissed her again, kissed her hard until she pushed him away.

"Bryce!"

He felt her reproach through the darkness. That would be God's way, to entrust a sensible girl like Amy with his divine will. Bryce sighed aloud and leaned back in the swing. "I ought simply to acknowledge my misfortune, I suppose. I believe in a God who is too deep for me. And I love a girl whose mind is always made up." He forced a laugh but stopped, abruptly aware that Amy was not contained in a word or two. She was new bread and honeycomb; she was morning. He had to have her. He rose and walked quickly off the porch.

"Amy," he said without turning. "Tell me again why." But he did not want her to and when she began he interrupted. "You love me. I know it. You love me and you won't marry me. I don't understand that. I don't understand this nonsense about going off to the academy either. You said once you didn't care about it any more." He leaned against the house, his arms folded tight against his body. "For God's sake, Amy, I'm in love! Don't you understand anything?"

If she had answered honestly she would have had to say no. She had never heard him use Deity that way. Perhaps if she married him right now as he wished she could help him never to profane again. But the simple fact was that she could not marry now. Yesterday she had been prepared to do so. Today she had been given two more years and she wanted them. But why? She lifted her feet a bare inch from the porch and let the swing go lightly back and forth. Every day as his wife she would make a visit to his prosperous father and stern mother. They were modest people, humble and frugal, but they were not like Ma and Pa. Was that her silly reason? She could cheerfully postpone forever the nameless, perplexing duty of a girl suddenly become bride, but if that was her reason it would not do either. Was it childbirth, about which she knew nothing except the cries of her own mother when Esther was born? The reason *must* be school.

"Amy, be fair to me. Be truthful."

"I do want to go to school, Bryce. And a married woman can't."

He came and sat beside her, taking her hand in his own. "When I get home I will be at least twenty-five, Amy. And you will be married to somebody else."

"Why, I never could!" Amy felt the clench of an invisible hand around her heart.

Bryce shook his head. He ought to scold his own impatience instead of this impossible girl. Whatever he did, he must not lose her. "Come on, my love, let's go inside. I want some of your ma's salt curd."

Amy watched his face for the rest of the evening without hearing a word he said to anyone. She would memorize the pale chestnut hair. The dimple in his chin she could remember easily. It was the exact size of her thumbprint. She watched him until his face turned bright red.

"Stop it, Amy," he said.

She laughed, "I see only one imperfection," she said, "and I will overlook that until we're married." She made up something foolish, as she had done many times before when he caught her staring. The truth was that she thought him perfect. And just as it had been easy to tell Alfred and Israel she was going to marry Bryce, it would be easy when she got to the academy to say, "I am promised."

How could Amy even suspect that by midsummer Bryce would release her from her vow? She knew nothing of how hurt and desire thrive on loneliness, of how a missionary could come to hate the cause of it all. A second letter from Boston came a few days after the first but was too late. "Amy," Pa wrote to Bryce, "will never marry you now. You have broken her heart and her spirit." Bryce had no alternative but to go back to knocking on the doors of the gentiles. Likely that was why Brother Taylor had written anyway, to get a missionary's mind on his work. At any rate, Bryce did not believe what Brother Taylor had said.

II

No new beaus came calling. Amy and Bryce had been a perfect match. Folks said that their industry, their talent, their integrity, their friendliness—the list went on—had predetermined a betrothal. This obvious fact demanded respect and got it—except from Israel Gordon. It demanded hesitation. Israel waited because he had to. When word got to him that Amy was free, he was thirty miles to the east tending sheep.

Hearing an outfit approach, he jumped from his wagon and ran toward the sound. He liked the loneliness of sheep camp partly because after a few days he could enjoy company so much. Sol Weeks climbed down and handed Israel a letter and a bucket of potatoes. "Just let me fetch some of that spring water, Brother Gordon, and I'll be going. Want to hit Goose Creek by dark."

"Couldn't you camp here tonight?" It had been two weeks since Israel had seen anyone.

"Maybe next time, but the horses ain't tired." He was already back to the wagon, his free hand extended. "Thanks."

"Goodbye, Sol." Israel lay the food inside and sat down on the tongue of his wagon. Deep into his mother's letter he read that Amy Taylor had been jilted. "Nobody is sure of the why's and wherefore's, but—" Israel dropped the letter and walked to the edge of the stream. From beneath the thin slice of spring water he took a rock washed clean and threw it hard into the sky. He did not watch it fall but took another, and another, and threw them high until his arm throbbed. Then he dropped to the ground. Lying on the rough gray earth, earth strangely colorless beside the red hills and mesas in the distance, he made up his mind to marry Amy Taylor himself.

Until that moment when she had told him she was to marry Bryce, he had thought no more about Amy than a dipped sheep. But the regard with which she had done that had struck Israel as the one virtue a woman ought to have. There was nothing personal in her gentleness; he could have been a June bug or a German count. But when she smiled and said "I'm promised" without the least conceit or curiosity, he remembered a forgotten spring day when they were both children. He had fallen from a tree and broken both wrists. "I'm sorry you got your arms broken," Amy had said, not as other children do when they covet a playmate's bandages, but sadly.

Israel had watched Amy go with feelings he had never felt before but with no resolve to win her back, as if he could, or even with a doubt that she would marry Bryce. He had simply hung his discovery in the back of his mind. Now he took it again and was pleased with himself.

But he could not leave the camp for at least a month and even then he might not be able to persuade his brothers to take over alone without giving them a better reason than courting Amy. After all, the girl had already given him the mitten once. The prospects when he did get into town would not be much brighter. He would have to go to dances and choir practices with a girl who danced and sang to perfection. Bryce Huntington's girl! Why, folks would say he was crazy! But he had no choice. The corn roasts would be all right; he could sit beside Amy in the dark and listen and watch the fire. And he could walk her from meeting in appropriate silence.

III

The courtship took Israel two years. While Bryce was preaching the gospel of Jesus Christ on the doorsteps of chilly Boston, Israel was moving his own cause forward—and backward. On his first trip to town to see Amy he escorted her to the Friday night dance, but after one tune he said he was sorry but he had had enough. He spent the rest of the evening looking on while Amy danced with the other fellows. He only stepped her one other time that first summer. As he walked her from sacrament meeting that evening, he learned that she was leaving for the academy the following morning. He told her he thought he would write to her if it was all right. She said she would answer.

Israel would have carried out his intention but when it came right down to deciding what to say he had nothing to say. He didn't think he loved her quite yet and had no notion of how to write a love letter anyway. His mother's newsy letters to sheep camp each summer were no help. He remembered his enjoyment but the news was a blur. What he needed were some facts and since he could think of only one fact important enough to write down—that he was going to marry Amy Taylor—and since he could not cross that bridge until he got to it, he let the winter pass in silence.

When he heard that Amy was home for the summer, he reminded his brothers that as the oldest unmarried son he had rights. "I will need to come into town every two weeks," he said.

"But she's Bryce's girl!" they pleaded. "Why waste your time and spoil our fun?" Israel went right ahead and planned their summer—and Amy's.

On the day of the young people's picnic at Strawberry Breaks, Israel took Amy to his family reunion at Indian Springs. Pa might not miss him unless he counted but since he always counted and since it was a count made not in judgment but in pride, Israel wanted to be in his proper place. Amy was disappointed to miss the picnic and might have said so but her disappointment was softened by anticipation. The reuniting of a polygamous family which except for this summer gathering was two families was an occasion. It made her long to be a child again.

A fort stood beside the pond, its high adobe walls a crumbling gray. Israel and Amy peered into the dark, silent rooms. Once outside, they wandered away from the food and the laughter toward where splashes of green clung to occasional springs. As they left all noise behind, Amy imagined that she was at sheep camp and could understand why Israel liked the quiet. She wanted to say so, but there was too much silence even for that. They stayed near the green, not talking. As they came toward a row of young poplars that grew along a shallow pond with sand reaching in on all sides, Amy saw one of the young trees sway and bend like a long bow.

"Hello! Hello!" An excited squeal came from the sapling and Amy saw a boy swinging back and forth, back and forth. She waved. "Hello!"

A few branches lay on the ground.

"That's Clara's son, isn't it?"

Israel did not answer.

"Hello, Is," squealed the boy.

"Get down, Charles," said Israel, and without looking at either the boy or Amy, Israel bent over the broken branches and laid them in a pile. "I said get down!" Charles jumped to the ground.

Israel stood there not moving, the moisture gathering in his eyes as if he were about to cry. He looked at his brother. Charles did not stir from his gaze but he did not meet it either, and when Israel took hold of him, one hand under each arm, he did not try to squirm free. Suddenly Israel lifted him off the ground and shook him hard until he bawled to get down. He shook him until Amy's own arms ached and Amy, unable to believe what she saw, started away. Israel called to her and as she came back he set Charles down. Then he hit him once across the cheek, knocking him to the ground.

"Now you let baby trees be!"

Charles nodded where he lay and started to get up. Before he could accomplish it, Israel picked him up and carried him to where the spring came out of the hillside. He took a handkerchief from his pocket, moistened it, and wiped the dirt from Charles' face. He did not notice that Charles was embarrassed. "Now, scoot!" he said, and the boy ran.

Amy wanted to run too. Instead, without knowing why, she followed Israel. He walked on ahead as if he were alone. When he finally sat on a boulder, Amy caught up with him and sat at his side.

"You needn't have hit him too."

Israel did not look at her.

"You hurt him!" Amy said, louder this time. She slid forward so that she could see his face and make him look at her. Tears still lay in his eyes.

"Israel!"

Now he looked at her. She had never noticed how deepset his eyes were or that they were gray. And she certainly had not known that he could get mad, especially at such a little thing.

"Are trees that important?"

He nodded. "Out here all life is important. Charles ought to know it."

"Will his mother be angry at you?"

Israel's answer came as if it were not an answer but a new subject that had nothing to do with her question. "Aunt

Regarding Courtship

Clara doesn't hit. Aunt Clara keeps your dessert or gives you a talking to. When Pa spanked us, she went out of earshot."

Israel looked over at Amy as if he were startled by being able to say what he wanted to say. "You're like her, Amy. Most ways you're like all the other girls, but—" He did not see Amy wince because words came pouring into his head as they sometimes did when he blessed a sick person and promised him health and prosperity and all kinds of blessings he didn't intend to.

"I like you because you remind me. When I was younger, I loved Aunt Clara more than I did my own mother. Our first summer down at Reservoir both families were living together. Aunt Clara got chills and fever so bad Pa decided to send her north. Pa asked me—I was nine and the oldest son he could spare—to drive the team and move her and her children. Charles wasn't even born then.

"I felt like a grown man all day driving the team and doing a man's work. She called me a man, too, but when night came and I built fires and had to make my bed under the wagon I was always a boy again. Aunt Clara and the children slept inside of course, but I lay all night under the wagon as a man ought to. Every night the wolves howled and whined and I knew I could not bear living until daylight.

"Once they came extra close. They were so near that I knew they would tear me to pieces. While I lay there too frightened to breathe, let alone cry out, I heard Aunt Clara's voice. 'Israel,' she whispered, 'would you like to come and get in the foot of my bed?' "

Amy thought she saw the tears coming again but they did not. "I vowed I would die for her if I ever got the chance." He looked at Amy. "You're gentle, too. Sometimes when you talk I don't hear what you're saying. I hear those same words, 'Get into the foot of my bed, Israel. Do you want to sleep at the foot of my bed?' "

Israel flushed and looked at the ground. Amy flushed too and they both laughed a little and walked some more without saying another word.

When they got back to the fort, the families were ready to leave. Israel drove his mother's wagon and sang louder than anyone else the songs that accompanied them across the desert. Amy did not sing. Was Israel courting her then? Did he intend to marry her? And if there were two of him—the awkward sheep tender without words and the eloquent but enraged defender of life, did she want either of them? When he asked her, she would say no.

IV

Israel did not give her the opportunity. At sheep camp he worried over the words (every day they seemed less presumptuous), but when he got into town he never let on. He took Amy to choir and to outings and he sat in her parlor and told Brother Taylor about the sheep situation, but he let the summer go by without speaking once of his intentions.

"Don't dawdle, Israel," said his mother. "She'll be off to the academy soon and before you see her again Bryce will be home. You're going to lose out if you don't quit dawdling."

The night before Amy was to leave, Israel was so tight with words he was even more silent than usual. When Amy got to talking an extra lot, nonsensically it seemed, he told her she was acting just like his emptyheaded little sister.

"I'm trying to make something pleasant to remember out of the evening."

"Well, then, be yourself. Don't talk every minute."

"You talk then. You talk for a change."

Israel turned toward her and took hold of both her hands. "I would if I could. I don't know why I can't unless it isn't time." He stood there looking at her and waiting for more to say. It didn't come. Quickly he kissed Amy on the lips for the first time, let her hands go, and turned and walked toward home. He felt as if he were walking into a gale and hoped that Amy could tell it and know that he did not like leaving her.

Israel asked his mother to go over his first letter and fix it up but after Amy's reply arrived he never went for help again. Just as anger had loosened a flood of words that day by a desert spring, Amy's letters loosed the poetry in Israel's soul. When she wrote that she must milk the cow morning and night and fix two meals for her board, he told her to guard her health for his sake and please not to overdo. When she wrote that she was down with rheumatism and had to miss two weeks of classes, he assured her that she must not worry. "I pray continually for your recovery and know that some day you will have no more rheumatism than anyone else." He was startled at his pleasure in writing her.

> "My own dear friend," he wrote. "It is with warmest interest in your welfare that I proceed to drop you a few lines. I can truthfully say that I am well and in good spirits. I hope this letter finds you enjoying yourself as well as myself if not better. I would be very pleased to have the privilege of accompanying you to meeting tonight.
> As ever, Israel H. Gordon"

When she returned from the academy he would be there waiting. Whether the sheep were watched or not he would arrange to be there. He would hold Amy in his arms, he would tell her he wanted to marry her. Then he would ask her if he could go to Brother Taylor for her hand. If it killed him, he would do it.

He did not know that Amy, moved to the edge of love by his letters, was dreaming the same dream. But he had forgotten all about Bryce and could not know that in Amy's dream the suitor kept changing. Whenever she planned her homecoming and what Israel would say the words belonged to Bryce. He had said them once and she could not think of true love being any other way.

V

Bryce arrived home tired, thinner, but even more assured and determined to have his girl. Boston had been a barren field for the Mormon missionary and there was new earnestness and shadow in his face as he told Amy that he hoped he had suffered enough for his mistake.

Amy wore the blue cashmere dress he had once given her and he brought her a brooch and a box of lace. She felt again the clenched hand around her heart.

"Don't say you will marry me yet, Amy," he said. "But give me a hope. At least let me try."

They sat in the swing and it was almost as if he had never left.

"You aren't promised to Israel, are you?"

"No, but I've been asked. He's waiting for my answer."

"Amy, he doesn't know anything about waiting!" Bryce started to rise, then sat back down. "I'm sorry I said that. It isn't his fault."

"No."

"Amy. Amy, will you put him off for one month? Will you wait to decide for just that long?"

"There was no one else to take the herd right now. He will be gone a whole month anyway."

"Let me come calling then. Let me come. Please, Amy!"

Amy leaned against the back of the swing and shut her eyes. Oh, say yes. Say *yes*. She raised her feet as she pushed and felt the lifting motion back and forward. How many nights after Bryce released her from her vow, then begged her forgiveness, had she longed for a moment like right now? She had forgiven him over and over in her heart though she had never written. Now here he was beside her and with a start she wondered how Israel in his extraordinary ignorance of how to win a girl had pushed Bryce aside. And what would he do to have her that Bryce couldn't do better?

"Amy?"

"I don't know."

"Do you love Israel then?"

The question surprised Amy. That was the question she had expected Israel to want answered, and all he had asked was her hand.

"No. I mean I don't know."

"Does he love you?" Amy smiled to herself. Israel had not even given her the answer to that question and the irony in it all left her feeling very strange. It was as if Bryce was doing for Israel what he could not do for himself.

"You don't talk like a girl who is ready to give her promise."

"Israel wants to marry me. He is set on it."

"Whether he loves you or not?"

It had occurred to Amy already that that may be exactly what Israel wanted, but she flared at hearing it said. "I don't think loving somebody, being sure of it anyway, is the most important thing to Israel. He feels love. He would die for Clara Gordon."

"But, Amy! I would die for you! I would give my life for *your* love!"

Amy put her feet on the porch and gently stopped the swing. She must not belittle such a declaration but she knew she must never, never extract it from Israel. Love was important, but so was life. Her mind spun. What was important? A tiny spring had made poplars grow in the desert. Maybe farms someday. Surely Israel's regard for her was a beginning of importance. And love or not, wolves or not, it was suddenly painful to think of him alone out there unanswered.

Bread and Milk

Amy looked at herself in the glass over the washbowl and saw Eve. She couldn't help it. Caught up in her miracle she would have been offended to remember that her own mother was a bride who had once kept the same astonishing secret.

Amy took the mirror from the wall, stood it against a jar of souring cream, and sat and looked at herself the whole time it takes mutton stew to simmer done. She touched her cheek, her throat, her sleeve. She reached for the sunlight by the window but it was out of reach, warmth on the wood floor. She pretended she dare not go get it. After all, she said to her image, we are going to be a mother.

She said it with her eyes because she could not yet say it with her voice, except to Israel in the darkest, quietest part of night, in a whisper. Even then her voice had been hesitant, and shy. And later, when she thought him asleep, Israel had said, "I saw it, Amy. I knew!"

She had stared toward him through the dark.

"I knew yesterday, by the way you talked. As if—as if you were afraid to breathe. It was like—"

Amy did not hear him finish. Her body numb, she could only lie there betrayed and relive one incredible, enchanted moment. No more than an hour before, uncertain how to tell a thing so fragile, so private, she had considered for one instant never sharing her secret with anyone. Her secret! With morning, intuition could be everywhere!

After Israel was asleep, Amy crept out of bed, tiptoed into the coolroom, and shut the door behind her. While she dug a wooden spoon full of firm honey, then let it melt on her tongue, she talked. She told herself that baby having was everyday, like bread and milk. She listened to Papa again: It is the pattern of all life in a world made out of joy and pains.

But could such a thing really be discerned in a voice? And if so, what was a bride to do? Her duty to a husband Amy had understood and accomplished. But to make it known without even meaning to do so, or worse, to acknowledge it by announcing her condition! It seemed as impossible as talking about an unanswered prayer.

The coolroom began to chill her. A decision had to be made. Well, if folks knew already, she would try to forgive them. If they didn't, they would not learn it from her. She would tell nobody, and she would remember to breathe when she talked.

Israel said he understood. "But we ought at least to tell your ma," he said more than once in the weeks that followed. They did not. Amy had forgiven him his presumptive eye in exchange for a promise.

Bread and Milk

And she was happy. To be alive was to be content. Every morning before breakfast, she went with her sweetheart along the trapline to look for red foxes, coyotes, and skunks. She got to weeping over the dead animals, but the strange weeping only increased her happiness.

"Your condition has made you foolish," Israel whispered one morning as they knelt over the trap and its victim. "I ought to leave you home."

But he never did. They drank from the bubbling springs fringed with watercress, they watched the sunrise as they climbed over the hills and through the brush. Evenings they trapped quail, dressed it, and hung it on a string before the hot coals of the fireplace to roast. Over parched corn, roasted apples and potatoes, they feasted and read and sang and told love stories. And all the time a secret thrived, twice protected; in Israel's heart it was a squirming captive, in Amy's, a friend, cushioned in light.

Lamps burn low, and go out. One Sunday morning Amy could not button her best bodice without a tug. Rushing to the mirror, she saw herself at last. She was not Eve. She was simply pregnant, and it would take a drunk Navee not to see it. Quickly she finished dressing, wrapped a shawl about her, and in her mind resolved to spend the rest of her life in the wood closet. Instead, she sat down and waited for Israel to finish hitching up the wagon. During Sunday School, she would think what to do. She would keep her shawl around her and she would think and by evening services, when she stood to lead the singing, she would have an answer.

"Go without me, Israel," she said as he came into the house. But she still wore her shawl and her plea sounded empty even to herself. "Please." Israel took her hands and led her through the door. "This afternoon I'll take you to see your ma."

As they walked into the chapel he took her hand. "Keep your shawl on, now."

Harriet Taylor put her arms around her daughter and held her. "Bless you," she said. "God bless you both, and now I have a surprise too." She disappeared up the stairs and was back with full arms.

"I will hold it up so you can see."

The mother hubbard was pale yellow, with an endless pattern of tiny black flowers. And it had full sleeves, the fullest Amy had ever seen.

"I was extravagant, Amy, but I couldn't help the sleeves."

Amy looked at it and away. "But Mama—"

"Amy. My dear Amy. Do I need to be told my daughter is going to have a baby? Forgive us. We tried to wait."

"Papa too?"

"Before I could tell Papa, he told me."

"Mama?"

"I think it was the way you walked, as if you were on fall leaves you didn't want to crush. Papa said you kept touching your cheek."

Amy sighed then, sank into a chair to cry, and would not let anyone touch her. Brand new in the world, like a newborn infant herself. That was what she was. And useless. How could she have forgotten that her own mother had had babies, maybe would again? And how could she keep up in a world where people did not need to be told the most secret of all secrets? Worse—oh, far worse—how could she await this baby, then bear it, with everyone watching, and later, helping? She stood up, dried her eyes, and walked to where the mother hubbard lay, a mound of sunlight. She wanted to understand.

"Everybody knows then, don't they. The Roskelleys and the Smiths and the—"

"They don't know, Amy, but they think they do because they expect it. Folks have been waiting."

"Waiting!"

"You have been married five months, you know."

Bread and Milk

Could it have been that long? Or had it been forever? Well, it did not matter.

"Mama, look at me. How can I stand up tonight in meeting and lead the singing before people who are waiting? How can I stand up there with my arms raised, my middle big and—"

"Amy!"

"I will look like a washboard!"

"Don't be vain, Amy. Remember—*all women have babies.*"

Amy could not explain nor discard her foolishness, how the thing she could not do was to help.

"I will have to stand up there and be weighed like a sack of grist."

"Yes, child, you will."

Amy stood clutching her shawl about her shoulders with one hand, the baton with the other. All eyes held her. How she had pleaded and coaxed on other Sundays: "Sit up straight, look high, keep up with the baton! Look at *me.*" Tonight not one face was toward the songbook in the lap. And everywhere she saw not friends and neighbors but only sinister curiosity. Israel was watching her too, but he was not singing. His favorite hymn and he was forgetting to sing. She clutched her shawl less tightly.

Amy made herself look into the faces, the intent, interested faces, and as she did she smiled. She could not help herself. In fact, if she did not do something right now, she would laugh.

She breathed deep as she tapped the podium with her baton. The music stopped. The voices faded. "Brothers and sisters." The shawl fell to the floor. So they would watch her, would they! So these blessed souls would wait for her to be with child, would they! "Brothers and sisters, you are forgetting that a song is a prayer."

She turned sideways, walked over to the window, and pointed into the black square of outside. "Do you hear the quail? Do you hear its cry? It is lonely. Now for goodness sake, sing as if you are lonely, lonely for the Father."

She walked slowly back to where she had stood, raised both arms high, and began to sing. Her father's face was a flush, her mother's a glow. All she could see of Israel was the top of his head.

Four and Twenty Blackbirds

The sun was a red hot pancake on Laun's shoulders. He squirmed. It clung. He caught a fly, let it tickle in his fist for a while, set it free. He watched sadly the big red ant making its roundabout way home across his toes. If Irma were husking too, he could drop it down her neck. Things being what they were, he sent the ant on home and husked another ear of corn. When he became a father, he would have a new saddle all carved and a shining shotgun. He saw them in his mind—waiting. He saw them in a wide cornfield without one ear of corn in it. In fact, there was not one ear, even husked, in the whole world. But Pa was there, uncomfortable, looking everywhere for the corn. Seeing Papa's face put a pinch in the boy's forehead; it idled his hands and his senses and he did not hear the wagon until it had stopped right in front of him.

"Laun!" Papa jumped to the ground. "What gets into you!" It was a judgment, not a question, so Laun did not reply. Israel piled the load of corn around his son in a circle of new hills. Laun worked feverishly then even though he knew that Papa was not looking at him but at how little corn had been husked. Laun had been bad, and again, for good reasons, it mattered like everything.

As Israel drove the team and empty wagon back across the creek his forehead tightened into rigid lines. Between his troubled eyes they deepened into a permanent pinch he did not even know was there. Day upon day from gray dawn to lamp-broken dark the demands on his physical body were too insistent for his mind to piece together even a complaint: You work too hard. Or a fancy: If there is corn to be husked in the kingdom of heaven, I will relinquish my tub full and go with the gentiles.

He stripped the stalks with sure, quick hands, his long back slightly bent. "Stock will have feed. The family will eat. Winter will—" But there were no conscious mind-workings any more except at prayer and on the Sabbath when his worship was total. Six days a week were industry. Industry in a man loved but worried after.

Some folks said that even if the Gordons had plenty, Israel would labor as hard as he did now. He would expect too much of his children, stunt their growth perhaps? Laun was so poor at liners that the other children taunted him. With pride and sorrow, folks remembered that pioneering and colonizing had taken the health of a whole generation. Give this generation and their sons and daughters long, healthy lives!

Israel Gordon did not have time to know what they said of him. Doing chores by lamplight, he even missed and never knew he missed the fanciful songs Amy sang as she put the children to bed. Small wonder he could not accept the absurdity of twenty-four blackbirds baked in a pie or understand how a nine-year-old could believe such a thing.

Aching under his pa's disapproval, Laun had forgotten the scalding sun. He husked for a long time, hours maybe, as if Pa were right there. He did not even see the blackbirds fly into Brother Nyman's poplars. But he heard something—a rustle? a caw?—and he looked up and there they were, hundreds of them, maybe millions. Sing a song of sixpence—blackbird pie. In an instant he was in the upstairs bedroom window, a 12-gauge shotgun with eight inches of its barrel sawed off aimed at a million blackbirds. Out of sight beyond them was Frank Nyman's front window.

Forty dead blackbirds slept in a community grave. Reimbursement promised, Frank Nyman snored soundly in his bed. Even Laun was in happy dreams despite an empty stomach and a sore bottom. Amy herself longed to rest and could have except for the tossing form at her side.
"Go to sleep, Papa. Please."
Sleep? We have a disobedient child and she wants to sleep? "If a child is working, he doesn't get into mischief, Amy. He should have been working. Why wasn't he?"
"I don't know. It is easier for some children to mind. And he wanted a blackbird pie."
"He wanted the corn to husk itself!" Israel sat up. "But it doesn't. Thank God it doesn't!" He sat stiff and silent and he thought. When an answer finally came he sighed and lay down.
"Amy, there is only one thing to do. When the corn is done, I'll take Laun up Main Canyon with a bunch of Grandpa's ewes and lambs. A week of herding will make the boy responsible."

Within moments Israel had gone to sleep. Amy was still awake when he went out to milk at five in the morning.

What *was* it about this canyon? Israel rode alone, hearing nothing in the wide dusk but silence itself, silence complete and kindly. As he arched the last hill the silence brushed his skin. Then suddenly like a whip descended the hundred months—maybe two hundred—that he had spent on these same hillsides. Out of them a mountain of memory distilled into sudden emotion. He straightened in the saddle and spurred the animal beneath him. To be the boy! To be becoming again! When he finally saw his son stacking firewood beside the wagon, he saw only himself, and for an instant would have died to make the vision true.

"Whoa. Whoa there!"

The boy whirled about.

"You won't need all that firewood, Laun. We're going home."

Laun still stood there, unmoving.

"It's me. It's Papa!" Israel stepped into the firelight and now the boy laughed and his arms were tight around Israel's waist. Israel looked about him. The pile of kindling showed care, attention to the chopping as well as the stacking. Through the wagon door Israel saw that the floor had been swept, the bed made, the old tear in the bed covering mended. In the doorway was the lantern, its chimney as shiny as a new dollar.

"Hey, hey now, son!" The boy would not let go. When had he hugged Israel last? or been hugged? Israel could not remember, but he let his fingers slide through the boy's hair and rest awkwardly on his shoulders. Every time Laun laughed aloud, he squeezed tighter and Israel knew he ought to say something loving. Perhaps he should chide the boy for being so strong or pretend to be suffocating. Instead he carefully freed himself and smiled down at his son.

"You're a sheep herder now, son. How are the sheep?"
"I didn't lose a one, Papa."
"Then why don't you make supper while I go look at them. All right? Have you beans cooked?"
"Oh, yes!"
"Good."

Israel saw the herd and knew the boy had become responsible. The two ate supper together, beans and biscuits and spring water. Israel felt good and he showed his pleasure. "Mama is fine. So are the little girls. Irma has eczema but she promises not to give it to you if you will come home."

Laun laughed again. "I don't think I can wait. It's like Christmas."

Israel stood. Yes, it was. He took his bed roll and flung it on the ground. "We better go to bed so we can make an early start for home." He spread out his quilts.

"Aren't you going to sleep in the wagon?"

"You're the sheep herder, Laun. The wagon is yours tonight."

"But, Papa, we can both sleep inside."

"I have my quilts, son. See? No reason to be crowded."

"Please, Papa. I won't wiggle. I promise. Please!"

Israel rolled up his bedding and they slept side by side, barely touching, on the narrow bed.

As they rode out at day break, Laun kept looking back.
"What is it, son?"
"We're leaving the sheep alone!"
"I told you. Grandpa will send someone for them."
"But, Papa! If he doesn't come right away—"
"Shhh. The sheep will be all right."

From the end of the street they saw Amy at the gate, and suddenly Laun was to the ground and running into her arms. Israel stopped at the corral. "He did well, Amy," he shouted. "Wait until I tell you!" He took care of the horse, then hurried smiling to where Amy and the boy stood. "Amy, this boy of ours, this boy—"

She was already nodding yes, an impatient, pleading nod for silence, but she was looking at the boy. Israel saw the moisture gather in her eyes. "Amy?" She did not answer. Laun clung to her but he was not squeezing and laughing as he had done the night before. Soft, reluctant sobs shook his body. Israel watched dumbly, his hands in and out of his pockets, his joy of a moment ago violated. Now Amy was on her knees beside Laun, pulling off his shoes, holding his blistered feet in the caress of those gentle hands.

Israel had not noticed the blisters. Why should he? Blisters were not hard to come by! But he saw them now. They were red and raw and pitted with dirt. Slowly he felt them, where he stood, and the pain became a memory. That first time out with the sheep you walked around them and around them, bundling them too much, fearing for them too much. From dawn to dusk you walked a circle, as if you needed to, for fear. You raised burning blisters by the dozens before experience taught you that you were foolish for it. Why hadn't someone told you? Because some things needed to be learned first hand to be understood. And they had to be learned gradually. "He'll learn, Amy! He'll learn it! He's *all right!*"

You walked and walked. Then you came back to camp and slept in your clothes. But before you slept you chopped more kindling than you needed. You mended bedding. You swept the floor twice and you lined up the cans and utensils in perfect rows. Last, last of all, you set to polishing the lantern chimney. Fascinated with its form, its transparency, you made it glow, hypnotized yourself into drowziness. Then you slept, still lonesome. Lonesomeness was a ghost in your wagon door in the middle of the night—or in the day—a constant painful surprise. The sunlight never sent it completely away.

Two long strides and Israel was bending over the boy. Touch him! Explain to him! Now!

But without doing it, Israel straightened and backed away. He was not this boy. Had his own ma needed to hold his feet, soothe them with his hands? Had she wept over him because he was pale? Had he cried? Why, this boy even howled if he got sent to bed without his bread and milk! Yes, herding was worse, but it was a kindness after all, not a punishment!

"Raise up, Laun. Come on now, Laun, *raise up!*" The boy did it, his eyes on Israel all the while. They were not the eyes of a friend.

Israel did not follow Amy and Laun into the house. He took the bucket from inside the screen porch and hurried to the barn. Molly was already calling to be milked and as he attended to her suffering, half-watched the warm, white arrows foam in the pail, he tried to lay his mind on a clear thought. "Sooooo. Sooooooo, Molly." He did not blame her for fidgeting. Tonight his hands were clumsy, as if they belonged to somebody else.

Israel frowned at his legs, legs so long he had to kneel to get comfortable on the milk stool, then fold them to the sides like chicken wings. His own pa wasn't all leg. Grandpa was sturdy, tight. And he was certain of his children. Before even one house had been begun at Willow Flat, before a one of his sons, hard as they worked, had an extra suit of clothes, his pa had sat one afternoon on the wide cook stove and said he wanted to talk. He always sat on the stove if the fire was out and if he had time to sit and if he had something to say to his family. The fire had never been built that day because it was reunion time and fixings for celebrations that big were always made the day before.

Papa had sat and leaned forward without even resting his elbows anywhere. Israel's knees were always in the way when he sat, demanding elbows, and at family prayer he had to kneel in the doorway to avoid cracking against the wall. But Papa had sat there as if pulled forward and held by his own strength. "I have a suggestion to make," he had said. "And it's a good one. It's right. We will start a town, have our own community. We'll build it down on the flat. Our children can have their own school and our women can have neighbors close enough for daily assistance and comfort. All right?"

Israel saw Grandpa sitting there surrounded by men who felt every one the claim a piece of ground put on him, men who had minded their pa, who had kept free of worldly temptation and idleness. Even before the first house was finished, the town had been named and the school block dedicated and cleared.

How did a man come by Pa's certainty? Some men had sturdy, tight bodies; some were lanky, long. That couldn't matter, could it? You had children. You reared them right or you didn't. If you didn't everything was nothing. Your own strength became a hand full of air, if not a mockery, unless your children were good.

For the first time in his life, Israel contemplated failure. He had seen it in the eyes of his son and he knew that a mistake had been made and that perhaps he—not Laun—had made it. But how? and when? He forgot Molly and the cumbersome knees and sank to the ground. Papa had nine sons. So far, he had one. Oh God!

When the sun had gone down and the milking and other chores had been completed, Israel walked back to the house. As he stepped inside he saw by the clock that Amy ought to be downstairs by now. The children ought to be asleep. But the kitchen and parlor were empty and from the top of the stairs he heard a note or two of a nursery rhyme.

Sayso or Sense

Amy Gordon was to have a new house, and in a frenzy of neighborliness folks came to tell Israel how to build it. Neighbors who shared work horses and yeast starts freely shared their wisdom. "If I were you, Brother Gordon—"

Too excited and pleased to do otherwise, the Gordons listened well; then after supper they separated the wheat from the chaff and fortified themselves for another day. Israel told Amy, "It's your house, within reason." Reason meant whatever the bank would loan a man with an excellent reputation and fair collateral. She was therefore careful with her dreaming: It would be a simple, strong house with plenty of room and one or two of those up-to-date advantages.

When Israel's father arrived—suitcase in hand—Amy showed him a cot in the children's room. "For as long as you will stay," she said. "Lola begs to sleep on the floor and she will have her wish."

"Thank you, Amy dear."

There were tears in the old man's eyes as Amy kissed him on the cheek. "We need you."

"I thought we would lay foundation today," he said, folding back his shirt cuffs.

Amy smiled and put her arm through his as they walked outside. "Oh, we're not ready for foundation, Grandpa. We've lots to do first." Sixty years experience, she thought. Sixty years head start. She watched him go, thankful in her heart for his strong back and, yes, even for his knowhow. What they did not want of it they could manage a piece at a time. The neighbors had given them plenty of practice.

But what are a few weeks of practice against a lifetime? Amy turned from her sewing and saw Israel and Grandpa, side by side, announcing before she was even aware of their presence that she did not want what she knew she wanted. In Israel's eyes was the zeal of a convert and in Grandpa's the patient kindness a good man shows the child found in error.

"You don't want a basement, Amy dear," said Grandpa.

How could she reply? Despite his size—he was six inches shorter than Israel—Grandpa had in his wide back energy for a full day's labor, in his hands the craftsman's skill. Worse, he had one of those rich, prophetic voices some of the Church leaders had, voices that didn't need to shout. And he had an iron gray mustache.

Amy looked at him and at the son who thought his father was Moses and wondered whether to go down fighting.

"Israel says it won't cost much more than an extra room upstairs, Grandpa. I do want a basement."

Sayso or Sense

"Amy, Amy, Amy," Grandpa's voice gradually softened, but it was the softening voice of intensity, not argument. You don't want one of those—those dugouts on this fine property!" He walked to the window. "What a fine corner lot! My—"

"But it wouldn't be a dugout, Grandpa. We'll have cement. It would be cool—and beautiful!"

"Amy." Grandpa came and put his arm around her shoulders. Still, he was not arguing. Still, his voice did not waver. "Amy, you need to be reminded that your own father—and I've known him all my life—was born in a cave on the side of a hill. I've heard him tell of it, how his pa dug that hole with his own two hands. But your pa never called it a house! It was a place to exist until a house could be built on top of the ground where a house ought to be. Do you think your pa didn't build that house as fast as he could?"

"Grandpa, there are no snakes here!"

He laughed without impatience. "I'm not talking about snakes, my dear. Why, an upstairs is heaven—and closer to heaven, too!" He smiled, his voice jolly and nostalgic at the same time. "My, but the mornings that come back to me out of an attic room with an east window. My, my—"

He was off into thought, as always, absolutely right, absolutely unmovable. But was he right? Amy looked at Israel for an answer but saw only Mosaic adoration.

"You promised me, Israel. We thought about a basement together."

"I know it, and we're not going to do anything you won't allow. But Pa has built a lot of houses."

"And now he's building ours?"

It was an unkind thing to say. No one in southern Utah could build a better. But her basement! She had felt its coolness, imagined the baby asleep there while she canned away August. She had already dug it with her bare hands.

Now Grandpa was rolling his sleeves all the way up, the matter settled. Of course it had been settled when he rode up with his suitcase. Amy would not have her basement. She would not have whatever Grandpa in a lifetime of experience had not found to be good. She could see her house now, just like Grandma Nellie's, with a steaming upstairs and deck porches the width of the house on both floors.

A carpenter came and Amy sent him to join the adversary. She tried to keep away from the window so she would not have to watch them bury forever her undug basement. Could she do as much? Could she bury her anger and never mention basements again as long as she lived? She could try. What did she really know about them anyway? A picture, a comment, things that wouldn't cover the head of a pin beside Grandpa's knowhow. She scolded herself, unselfishly took all the blame for troubling the waters, and hoped for an extended peace, hoped that Lola had not outgrown that old whim of hers about sleeping on the floor.

By the time the foundation was laid and the plans were completed, Amy had given up her ample closets: "Can't you see that they would encourage the foolish acquiring of clothing? Remove temptation. Be frugal and simple, my dear." She had also changed her mind about wanting deeper, more gradual stairs: "A waste of space, daughter. Up is up." But these submissions were trifling. Amy began to suspect male judgment in any form. If Israel said, "Bedtime," she got to looking at the clock, even if she was having difficulty keeping her eyes open. When he called on one of the children to say family prayer—no matter who it was—she knelt there wondering whose turn he had overlooked. But the thing that finally shattered her faith in men, the thing that finally made Grandpa an old man with old-fashioned ideas, was the problem of which direction the house ought to face. Only it was not a problem to Amy. She had never for one second seen it as a matter that needed deciding until she overheard the men talking.

"Will the house look west or south, Brother Gordon?" asked the carpenter.

Grandpa was silent, and silence made Amy uneasy. West. To the main road of course. To the west!

"How fortunate to be on a corner lot and have a choice." Grandpa sounded really grateful. "By all means," he said, "the main entrance should be on the south."

South? Amy looked over at Grandpa and in a tight, slow voice said, "Why don't you put it on the roof?"

"What was that, Amy dear?" asked Grandpa.

"I'm sorry, Grandpa. I was being foolish. I thought I heard you say that the house was to face south."

"By all means."

Amy sat down and picked up her mending, but her trembling hands would not sew. She had been patient. She had been agreeable. Sometimes she had been right. And all those times floated back, giving her strength.

"By *what* means, Grandpa? By *what* means? Why south?" She stood and went to the door. South she saw the cemetery, the narrowing road where it curved into the desert. South she saw one house: the shanty where Watermelon Joe lived.

"Look south! Look!"

"The town is going to grow, Amy. Someday the main part of town will be out there."

"It will?"

"It will."

"But, Grandpa! The school, the church house, the store, the people! They're all north! The whole state is north!" She looked at Israel. "Don't let him!" Back to Grandpa. "What isn't north, Grandpa? Name one thing that isn't north!"

The carpenter filled the silence. "That's just it, Sister Gordon. North is all filled up. North is utilized, fully utilized."

"That's why a south front would be nonsense. Don't you see? Everyone who comes, including our children and ourselves, including you, Grandpa, on your way from Willow Flat, comes from the north." She sat down again. "My garden and kitchen are on the north. Folks will spy the back door and they will come right in. Who will walk clear around the house just to get in right? Everyone will come through my kitchen—the bishop, the Relief Society sisters, the apostles!"

Amy was sure she had been convincing. She would forgive Grandpa his momentary blindness. After all, he had built most of his houses where there were no main streets to consider. She smiled at him and he smiled back.

"This decision is very important. You will live here for the rest of your lives." It was an observation, not a rebuttal.

"That's true, Grandpa."

"You will likely never move again. You ought to be content."

Sometimes she loved that voice.

"Yes, Grandpa. You do see." Perhaps he *was* a Moses.

"And when the town grows south—"

Amy felt her cheeks flame. Had he heard one word?

"When the town grows south, a west entrance will be a daily annoyance, a daily reminder of lack of foresight. When the—"

"When! When! When!" She was sure she would cry. "And when the town does not grow south, I will have a daily annoyance that will drive me out of my mind!" She ran from the room, abandoning the men to their visions. She could see the town through her tears, snuggled against the graveyard, the rattling homestead, the barren fringe of desert. She would *not* submit!

But that night she had a dream. God was conducting priesthood meeting and Grandpa and Israel and the carpenter were on the front row, hanging on every word. God said when they came to earth, men could have their choice—sayso or sense—but they couldn't have both because that wouldn't be fair to the women. He called a vote and Grandpa's hand shot up for sayso before God had finished speaking. Amy awoke, sure the choice had been unanimous.

By daylight she had decided that, God approving, she had no alternative but to leave the men to their folly.

After breakfast she made her speech. "The front door should face west, main street. It should be easy and logical to get to from the north. Or the south. My mind is the same as it was last night. However, I gave up my basement, which would have been cool and beautiful, and I gave up my vain closets and wasteful stairway. I will now give up having my front door on the front of the house."

"Amy, Amy, Amy."

"I don't want to talk about it any more."

They left her, their stomachs full, their minds undoubtedly troubled that she did not see. Perhaps Israel reminded his pa that it was Amy's house after all. But Amy never even hoped it. She let herself be mad inside whenever she wanted to and she watched them build her house the way they wanted to. She never let on what she had dreamed or how much she hurt inside. When they built her a coolroom with several inches of cobble rock underneath the cement floor and with sawdust between the studding in all the walls, she showed them her pleasure. Inwardly she marveled at how the men in her dream could go about building such a fine coolroom without her objections.

But to nurture such sarcasm made Amy uneasy. It was wrong for a woman. When the house was finished, the pictures hung, the rooms moved into, she was pleased, and she longed to have once more her sturdy faith in Israel, that trust that made obedience beautiful. She longed to feel again that the priesthood could actually carry the burdens without throwing the world into chaos.

When it came time to dedicate the new house to the Lord's care, Israel relinquished his right and asked Grandpa to offer the prayer. Amy hid her unsightly wash boiler and such things as usually hang beside a back door, and on Sunday afternoon Grandpa and a radiant band of friends and neighbors filed in through the kitchen. They arranged themselves in the parlor.

As Grandpa began to pray, Amy's heart churned for a miracle. She had to have it! "Father, we dedicate into Thy watchcare and keeping this beautiful home." *Oh Father, it is beautiful, it's beautiful regardless!* "Bless this good family. Thou knowest the intents of their hearts are righteous, Father." *Thou knowest how men are, Father. Help me to take no delight in their folly.* "Bless every comfortable room, bless every child who grows there. Bless the timbers that the elements—" *Bless me never to mention my basement again. Remove bitterness, doubt.* "Within these walls let Thy Holy Spirit abide in peace always, we pray Thee, in Christ's name, Amen." *In peace. In peace. Oh, please! Amen.*

Amy sank into a chair. Not until Grandpa came over and looked into her eyes and took her hands between his own did she realize she was still crying.

"Thank you, Grandpa."

"I'm sorry everybody invaded the woman's realm by tracking through the kitchen, Amy dear, but please don't cry."

She cried harder.

"My, my, Amy. It's only a house," he said.

Amy's eyes were suddenly dry. She looked up at the old man.

"Of course, Amy. A worldly convenience. Trivia is trivia and must remain so in a world of sorrow."

Amy's heart quieted after that. Oh, there were setbacks. The President of the Church himself walked through her kitchen once during soap making, and one cold Saturday night the Relief Society sisters almost stumbled over Israel sitting before the oven door in the bathing tub. There may even have been another time or two when Amy came so near telling Israel her dream that she trembled. But she kept it. Trivia is trivia. Besides, how could a dream matter to Israel when it made less and less sense to her.

God Willing

Amy had her first heart spell at three in the morning and she lay there waiting to die in a turmoil of ecstacy and disappointment. By dying now she could go to Israel suddenly and in one piece. She wouldn't have to dodder through endless pains and restrictions and finally die too worn out to enjoy their meeting!

But the thought of being gone brought a huge sadness. The great grandchildren were just beginning to come along. What would become of them? Would they bolt in and out of her porch swing, fly through these rooms searching for her? Of course they wouldn't. If they came at all they would approach the yard one step at a time: Grandma Amy? Who was she?

Amy lay still as stone, indecision flapping like wings around the heart where pain seized, pushed out, rested. Oh, poor children! And why couldn't she remember whether to let air in or out, if indeed she was still breathing? Poor children! Please help them. Lola is so busy, and tiring already. Irma too. Oh, their poor babies to have no Grandma Amy!

"You're an egotist, Dear. Better to say poor Israel dead all these years and tired of waiting for you."

She heard herself say it and opened one eye, then the other. She was alive.

When daylight finally came the pain had left and there were noises of present children through the window. Amy lifted herself from the bed. She made oatmeal mush and walked out the kitchen door and down into the garden eating it. Perhaps she shouldn't weed this one morning. For the great grandchildren's sake she ought to be careful. And she ought to sit down to eat.

She turned around and walked back up to the house. She washed her dish and spoon and lowered herself into a chair by the kitchen table. Yes, the pain really was gone. She had been given time. Staring into the white of the table cover, Amy whispered, "How much? Please, how much?" Was there time for more great grandchildren? Maybe. Time to feel offended about dying? Probably not. But she couldn't bear becoming a stranger to all those children. She stood up, took the pencil and notebook from the cupboard drawer, and sat down again. Then she began:

"That my own children and children's children might know me, and the ways of life common to my time, I record the following—"

"Grandma! Jess has the swing going and won't stop so I can get on. Grandma, come and make him stop! Grandmaaa!"

The yell faded but Amy was already on her feet and out the front door as if she were well to make Jess either share or go weed half a row of onions. Poor children! Jess moved over of course but Amy went back inside trembling and melancholy. Why had she grabbed the swing, and even shaken the pencil in Jess' face? Was that necessary? How were they to become acquainted with their old friend mortality if she kept smoothing things out for them? She must think, darn it! She mustn't make life too soft.

Amy sat down fluttering, breathing, longing to know how much. Now where was she? She squeezed the pencil, pointed it against the paper, and she was not where she ought to be. She was watching Israel. She ought to be on page one telling how it was the summer she was born and how not doctors but midwives did the honors in those days. She ought to begin at the beginning if she could. But there was her beloved Israel hanging over the brass frame along the foot of the bed, leaning and pushing his stomach against the cold hard round surface and saying with moist eyes that he thought the pushing did help.

The day the great pain lifted itself free, Israel told Amy to get the pencil and paper from the drawer and write down his funeral program as he told it to her. Amy sat against him on the bed instead of in the chair because he insisted. Her weight there didn't hurt him, he said. She squeezed the pencil and wrote out word for word who was to pray and who was to preach and what about and what the choir was to sing. His words came steady and warm, like heartbeats.

"Talk on pre-existence, beauty of it, God's plan in having it that way, Brother Willard Mackelprang. Talk on purposes of life, what we can do here to enter celestial glory, President Seegmiller. Take charge, Bishop Ronald Chamberlain. Family prayer at closing of casket, Tom Weeks. Dedication of grave, Fred Carroll. Prayers at funeral, Asa Judd and John Wilson."

"Now the singing. 'I'll Go Where You Want Me To Go, Dear Lord,' choir." At first Israel spoke calmly, as if he had thought about his funeral all his life, but now Amy felt his body become taut in the bed. She clung to the pencil.

" 'Farewell All Earthly Honors,' choir. 'God Be With You Till We Meet Again,' choir. 'Oh What Songs of the Heart We Shall Sing All the Day,' priesthood brethren Julius Dalley, Merrill Tietjen. Leo Chamberlain. Reed Cramer. John McAllister. Ray Young."

As the heartbeat of names ended, Israel sank back against the pillow and shut his eyes. "Brother Mackelprang is a true saint," he whispered, as if to answer Amy's silent protest that he certainly wasn't a very good speaker. Then Israel slept. When he finally opened his eyes, the fire in them astonished Amy. "The only good thing about a funeral is preaching and music," he said. "I don't want flattery. I want the gospel preached!"

What Amy wanted to say to him and couldn't was that he looked stronger! Perhaps— But Israel went on, each word now a strenuously born whisper. "Sorrow is private. Between two people. At most, two people." He looked toward Amy and reached out. She took his hands. She could feel their hardness now, like bare bone. "Funerals are too fancy, but— getting out of one— would be— hard," he said.

Amy nodded. She was nodding now, and the porch swing was creaking and her heart was rolling under a slab of steel.

"Come, come Amy. "I'll— be— by you."

Amy sprang to her feet and hurried out the back door. Grabbing a hoe and dragging it along behind her, she trotted down the corral path to the garden. She pulled her hoe into the dirt again and again until at last she was able to think of the carrots and potatoes taking shape in the ground. She would like to wait, God willing. She would like to harvest the vegetables and just a few more great grandchildren. If she could put her memories in order and sort them out, she would like time to write them down! But

God Willing

she would have to forget Israel's suffering and the severity of widowhood. Oh, why did memory have to be ungovernable, like Lola's boy? Some memories were welcome, of course, like company! You shined the best dishes for them, sat down close after feasting and listened and listened and gathered all the pleasure you could. As for others, well, they crashed off with you like a runaway team pulling a hay wagon.

Amy sat on the ditchbank and let the sun wrap around her and reach into her bones. Another hot day coming on. She might need to take off her stockings. Lola's boy would turn out all right. Probably he would. Right now he was contrariness in flesh.

Amy was careful. She didn't weed anymore, or sweep, and she tried to hold her memories tight. She did take off her stockings, though she hated that chore. Sweeping would have been easier on the heart. To ease her conscience about the swing, she gave Jess ten cents to go uptown and see if she had any mail. Then she wrote down what she had been told about the day of her birth. She ought to write down those childhood experiences next, the ones that came at night when the house was still and everyone else in the world was sleeping. There were funny times. What were they? But every time she loosed her memory it shied and bolted. It brought the bank to the door, pressing for payment, that incredible day the sawmill caught fire, sending their dreams of freedom from debt up in smoke. It even brought again that offended, misused feeling she got the day the cows harvested the pea crop. Her mother would have said, "No great loss without some small gain. They saved you a back-breaking job."

Amy lay back in her rocking chair and shut her eyes. Life had no sequence any more. It had become one enormous recollection, and today it was showing its bad side. "All right," she sighed. "Get it out of your system. Have your fling, and then I'll settle down to business."

It was at the meal after the funeral and Olive and June were worrying across Amy's lap about what Israel, newly dead, was doing. They sat on each side of her, leaning over their plates.

"I hope they've got him doing something. He was the most nervous creature I ever saw when he wasn't doing something."

"The scriptures say if you're good, you get to rest."

"But Israel wouldn't! He'd be miserable!"

"The question is, would they make a person rest."

"They'd have to make Israel. Otherwise—"

Amy saw an enormous *they* in robes sitting on Israel's lap holding him down. Israel did look miserable. Olive slid closer and put her arm through Amy's.

"You lived with Israel for thirty years. Is he resting or working?"

It was easy for Amy to imagine her beloved walking into a gathering of Gordon ancestors he hadn't seen for ages and asking where the work was. But she also knew that it might take more than dying to kill his appetite for family reunions.

"Oh, he's probably at a doings," she said. "There are tables like these heaped with food and surrounded with family." She smiled at her two friends. "Aunt Hannah is saying what a shame it is someone has to die before they get together!"

The laughter that followed was affectionate and free and Amy went on. She couldn't help herself. "He's probably telling Aunt Hannah how good it looks to see her sitting all the way down. He never saw her sit square in this life. You can't cross the plains on a mule and a broken hip and heal right. I suppose even Israel has got to visit before life can settle down to normal."

The three women talked in subdued tones, concocting eternity out of the familiar, like doings after a funeral, and then the visions faded into tears and finally Amy started to cry. There was something real there that day, everyone eating, talking, being glad for an excuse to be together. For honesty it beat grief a mile. It was truth beside pagan ritual. When Olive and June went back for more casserole, the others, each, one at a time, slid into a chair on either side of Amy and touched her and listened to her and said thank goodness for our knowing separations are temporary.

When the doings were over Amy was so exhausted, so completely tired, that she had no idea she would live these twenty years.

The clock said the day was half gone. There was the refrigerator, clear across the room. Cupboard dishes would require reaching. Amy decided to wait a while to eat. If the boys were still on the swing she would tell them to get her something. Besides, she wanted to tell them it was a good life. But the swing hung quiet. Perhaps she would rock, and rest, and after while—. She tipped back and forth, back and forth. Why, she hadn't taken that leisure for ages!

Shhh— Shhh— Poor children! "Waiting in the rain. Waiting in the rain. I never shall forget—" Larry was on her lap singing after her the sad-ending love song only Grandma Amy knew. He was not sleepy.

> Waiting in the rain
> I never shall forget
> The day that I stood waiting in the rain
> You are the one who has to decide
> Whether you'll do it or toss it aside
> You are the person who makes up your mind
> Whether you'll lead or linger behind.

Suddenly grown, Larry was the tallest, and Fred the one with enormous freckles and slicked curls. John's face was pale as his white hair, for fright, and Roy stood tipped forward of the others as if to meet his turn head on.

Nobody here will compel you to rise
No one will force you to open your eyes
No one will answer for you yes or no

Four grandsons, four young men with young jaws showing signs of bony manhood and fuzz. Each stood there framed in crysanthemums and ribbons and fern and stiffly recited his verse without one slip-up. Amy trembled seeing it again because the excitement of that moment had put a permanent flaw in her bones. Those scared, half-grown, unknown quantities, not quite spitting images of their dads or any other human creature, not happy about their grandad dying but not unhappy either. There they stood and the way of their standing, awkward as it was, sent praise to heaven, praise for the dead man whose blood flowed in their veins and whose stature added height to theirs.

"I don't want flattery. I want the gospel preached!"

Amy winced. "Well, the doctrine was pure, Israel. And the boys, too, as you probably know. And they still are. Could I help it if they were strong looking, handsome boys? If it was praise it was sideways praise, and honest. It didn't come from anyone's mouth.

"Well, yes, I did change the program. No, not changed—enriched, embellished. Your part was good too, but these were the best of the Taylors and Gordons. Our offspring!

"The dollars? Oh, Israel, for goodness sake, a silver dollar isn't much for thirty-two lines of poetry and if I hadn't paid them they would have read it!

"The blood was there so of course the tribute to you was there, but Sweetheart, that day I saw glory! I saw an eternity of sons!"

Why not? Oh, why not? She could still feel Laun's big shoulder on one side of her at the services, Alma's arm along her back, holding her so tightly against him she could feel his heart beat. They were mountains that day, steadying her, lifting her away from her brief loss. Israel was not dead! In spite of funerals and what the loneliness of her night, and trouble, said to her, hadn't she looked out the window uncountable times these twenty years and seen Israel hoeing in the field? Could that *really* be Laun?

"You will have power and influence with your offspring and will have wisdom given unto you at all times to counsel and direct them in righteousness." Well, she had done what the patriarch promised she would. She had. Of course Larry had married that flighty Webb girl anyway, but she had turned out better than expected, and would still improve with experience. If Amy could stay out of their quarrels the great grandchildren might turn out too. From now on, if they fought over the swing, she would let them work it out without her meddling.

Which is about what things had come to anyway. Life had turned from doing to being done for. Why, she couldn't even mend a fence anymore—or didn't get the opportunity—for being done for.

Amy took the pencil and began to write. There was a numbness in her arm, slight but not imaginary. She wrote regardless, driven to preserve the picture and the point of the four boys. When she was finished, she fell backward. Then she let go of the pencil. "Please," she said aloud. "I want the memory about my wedding day!" She was in her white dress, waiting, and Israel hadn't come yet. She started to cry and there he was, arms outstretched, hurrying toward her. Only this time, the hair and mustache were white.